'I wish my tail was that colour,' said Snowie the dog. 'I hate being all white, and Snowie is such a silly name.'

'Well, it's just as bad being all black,' said Cinders. 'It's very dull. Now if I were striped yellow, I should feel grand.'

'Will you have any paint left over when you have finished your job, Ho-Ho?' asked the dog.

'I might,' said Ho-Ho. 'But if you think I'm going to waste it on you, you're very much mistaken.'

'Yes, but the chancellor would be so pleased,' said Cinders. 'I'm sure he's tired of seeing us all one colour. He might pay you double for being so kind.'

'I don't know about that,' said Higgle-dy. 'I've heard the chancellor isn't very generous.'

'Snowie! Cinders! Come and have your dinners!' called a voice. The two animals ran off and Ho-Ho and Higgledy went on with their work.

The next day and the next Snowie and Cinders came and watched the two brownies, and on the third day, when Ho-Ho had finished painting the walls a beautiful bright yellow, and Higgledy had made a very nice bookcase, the two animals went over to the paint tin. They looked into it and then spoke to Ho-Ho.

'Ho-Ho, *do* let us have the little bit of paint that's left,' begged Cinders. 'We would be glad of it and we are sure the chancellor would be pleased. Couldn't you just paint us yellow with your big brush? Do! Do!'

'Please!' said Snowie, wagging his tail hard. 'How would you like to be dressed in nothing but white all your life?'

'I shouldn't like it at all,' said Ho-Ho. 'But I don't know whether I dare to do what you want.'

The animals begged so hard that at last Ho-Ho and Higgledy gave in. Higgledy painted Snowie's long tail a most beautiful yellow, and gave him yellow ears too, and Ho-Ho painted long yellow stripes all down Cinders' black body.

THE ENCHANTED GLOVES

They did look funny. Ho-Ho and Higgledy began to laugh when they saw how strange the two animals looked. But Cinders and Snowie were pleased. They ran out of the room and down the passage, and just round the corner they met the chancellor.

He stared in astonishment and horror at his cat and dog. Whatever could have happened to them? Was this really Snowie, with yellow ears and tail? What a horrible-looking animal! And could this really be his beautiful black cat Cinders, with long yellow stripes down his body?

'My eyes must be going wrong!' groaned the chancellor. 'Where are my glasses?'

He put them on and looked at the animals again – but they were still the same. What a terrible thing!

'Who has done this dreadful deed!' roared the chancellor, suddenly feeling very angry. 'Ho-Ho and Higgledy, is it you?'

He strode into the dining-room and found the two brownies there, looking rather scared.

'How dare you paint my cat and dog!' shouted Long-Beard. 'Get out of my palace at once!'

'But please, sir, Snowie and Cinders begged and begged us to,' said Ho-Ho, trembling. 'We didn't want to do it, but they said you would be pleased.'

'I don't believe you!' said the chancellor, angrily. 'You did it for a horrid joke. Go away at once and never come back!'

'We've finished our work,' said Ho-Ho, 'so we will go if you will kindly pay us, sir.'

'Pay you!' cried the chancellor. 'Not a penny piece! Not a penny piece! Ho there, servants! Come and throw these wicked brownies out.'

Two servants at once ran up, caught hold of the brownies, and threw them down the front steps of the palace. Ho-Ho and Higgledy picked themselves up and ran off in fright leaving behind all their tools and brushes.

They didn't stop running till they came to Sunflower Cottage. Then they sat down in their little chairs and wept bitterly.

'Nasty, horrid old chancellor!' said Ho-Ho. 'We did our work. Why couldn't he have paid us? He just wanted to save the money, the mean old thing!'

'We'll pay him back somehow!' said Higgledy, drying his eyes. 'We'll go to Thumbs, the glovemaker. He's very clever and perhaps he will think of some way to punish the mean chancellor.'

So next day they went to visit their friend, Thumbs. He made gloves – red ones, white ones, brown ones, blue ones, little and big, thin and thick. He was very clever indeed.

'Welcome!' he said, when he saw his two friends. He put down his work and set out three mugs and three plates. 'We will have some biscuits and cocoa. You look sad. Tell me your trouble.'

So over their steaming mugs of cocoa, Ho-Ho and Higgledy told Thumbs all about the mean chancellor and how he had thrown them out of the palace without paying them a penny, just because they had been kind enough to do what Snowie and Cinders had begged them to.

'We mean to punish the chancellor, but we can't think how to,' said Higgledy. 'You are clever, Thumbs. Can you help us?'

Thumbs put his finger on his nose and rubbed it, thinking hard. Then he began to smile.

'I've got an idea!' he said. 'It's old Long-Beard's birthday next week. I'll make him a pair of gloves and you can send them to him without saying where they come from. Inside the gloves I'll put a naughty spell. This spell will act as soon as he puts the gloves on.'

'What will it do?' asked Ho-Ho in excitement.

'Why, it will make him pinch, punch and pull anybody who happens to be with him at the time!' said Thumbs. 'Both his hands will act so strangely he won't know what is happening! They will pull people's noses, box their ears, tickle their ribs and pinch them! Goodness, how funny it would be to watch!'

Then Ho-Ho, Higgledy and Thumbs began to laugh till the tears ran down their noses and dropped into their cocoa. Oh, what a joke it would be!

THE ENCHANTED GLOVES

All that week Thumbs worked at the gloves. They were beautiful. Each was deep red and had little yellow buttons. They were edged with white fur and were quite the loveliest gloves that the brownies had ever seen.

When the right day came Ho-Ho and Higgledy posted the parcel to Long-Beard. They had decided that they would take a walk near the palace on the afternoon of the chancellor's birthday, to see if they could find out what had happened.

THE ENCHANTED GLOVES

Long-Beard had scores of parcels on his birthday. He opened them one after another, and most of them he didn't like a bit for he was a mean old man. But when he came to the gloves – oh my! What a surprise! What magnificent gloves! How warm! Who could have sent them? There was no card in the parcel and Long-Beard puzzled hard to think who could have given him such a nice present.

'It must be the King himself!' he thought at last. 'He thinks a lot of me, and I expect he has sent me these gloves to show me how much he likes me. Well, I must wear them this afternoon, that's certain, for the King is calling for me in his carriage, and he will like to see his present on my hands.'

So that afternoon, at exactly three o'clock when the King's carriage rolled up, the chancellor stood ready to join the King. He carried his new gloves in his hand and he meant to put them on as soon as he was in the carriage, and then the King would see them and perhaps say that he had sent them.

THE ENCHANTED GLOVES

The carriage came and the King leaned out to greet his chancellor.

'Come into the carriage, Long-Beard,' he said. 'It's a beautiful afternoon for a drive.'

Long-Beard stepped in and the door was closed. Just then up came Ho-Ho, Higgledy and Thumbs, out for their walk near the palace. When they saw the chancellor getting into the King's carriage with the enchanted gloves, they stood still in fright. Whatever would happen to the King when Long-Beard put on his gloves?

'Come on, we must go with the carriage!' cried Ho-Ho, and he ran after it. All three brownies swung themselves up on the ledge behind the carriage and sat there, unseen by anyone.

The chancellor put on his gloves and the King looked at them.

'What beautiful gloves,' he said – and then he gave a shout of surprise!

Long-Beard's hands had suddenly flown to the King's nose and pulled it hard! Then they went to the King's ribs and began to tickle him!

'Ooh!' cried the King. 'Ooh! Stop it! Whatever is the matter with you, Long-Beard? Have you gone mad?'

The chancellor was horrified. What was happening? Why were his hands doing such awful things? Now they were boxing the King's ears! He tried to put them into his pockets but he couldn't.

They flew to the King's head, knocked his crown off and pulled his hair! Then they slapped his face and pinched his cheeks as well!

The King grew angry and slapped the chancellor back. Then he gave him a punch that made him gasp. The three brownies saw all that happened for they were peeping in at the windows, and they were horrified.

'Gloves, come to me!' cried Thumbs, suddenly.

At once the red gloves flew off Long-Beard's hands and went to Thumbs. The chancellor's hands stopped behaving so strangely, and he stared at the King in shame.

The King stopped the carriage and got out. 'I must get to the bottom of this,' he said. 'Can you explain it, Long-Beard?'

'No, Your Majesty, I can't,' said Long-Beard, trembling. 'I don't know how it happened at all.'

'Well, perhaps *you* can tell me the meaning of this!' said the King, turning suddenly to the three brownies who stood near by, red and ashamed.

'Please, Your Majesty, I will confess everything,' said Ho-Ho, and he told the King all that had happened – all about the work done at Long-Beard's palace, the cat and the dog painted yellow, and the chancellor's anger and meanness. Then he told how Thumbs had made the gloves to punish Long-Beard and the King looked stern.

'You had no right to think you could punish the chancellor yourselves,' he said. 'You should have come to me and made your complaint. You have done wrong and you must be punished. As for the chancellor, he did wrong too, but he has been punished enough. He must certainly pay you what he owes you, but you must give half of it to the brownies' hospital.'

The three brownies agreed, and then the King forgave them. The chancellor opened his purse and with very bad grace gave Ho-Ho and Higgledy the money he owed them.

'You might give me ten pounds to put in the hospital box, too,' said the King to the angry chancellor. 'I'm sure it wouldn't hurt you.'

Then the carriage rolled off again and the three brownies walked home, not knowing whether to be glad or sorry.

'We'd better not be naughty any more,' said Ho-Ho at last. 'What do you think, Higgledy and Thumbs?'

'We think the same,' said his friends. So for quite half a year they were as good as gold – and after that – ah, but that's a different story!

Pixie Pockets

Once upon a time Snippit and Trim, the two pixie tailors, were very upset because someone had come in the night and taken all their needles and their best pair of scissors. Their reels of thread were gone too, and they were in a great state because they had promised to finish a suit for the King that day.

'We've got another pair of scissors,' said Snippit, 'but we have no more needles and no more thread. What shall we do?'

'We might ask the spider for some more thread,' said Trim. 'She has plenty to spare.'

So they sent a messenger to ask the spider, and she came to them and let them draw enough thread from her to fill two reels. She caught six flies in their shop, and that was her payment.

'What about needles?' said Snippit. 'We do need such fine ones for this important work.'

'Zzzz!' said a big bee who had blundered into the shop, thinking that the fine blue suit the pixies were making was a bright flower. Snippit was just going to shoo her out when he thought of a clever idea.

'Wait a minute, Bee!' he cried. 'Will you do us a favour?'

'Zzzz! What izzz it?' buzzed the bee.

'Will you give us your sting to use for a needle?' begged Snippit.

'What will you give me in return, Sssnippit?' buzzed the bee.

'Anything you want,' said Snippit. 'Let us have your sting and you can think of something. We will make you a coat – or a vest – or a new belt.'

'I'll think for a while,' said the bee, and she let Trim pull out her sting very carefully. Then she went to fetch a friend, so that both little tailors might have a needle and work together.

The bees sat and watched the busy pixies and marvelled at their sewing. The stings made fine needles, and you should have seen Snippit and Trim sewing with them, making tiny little stitches with the spider-thread.

When their work was finished they turned to the patient bees. 'Have you thought of anything you would like?' asked Trim.

'Yesss!' buzzed the first bee. 'I have thought of something we need very badly. We want pockets to put the pollen from the flowers in. We collect that as well as honey, you know. Could you make us pockets, pleazzze?'

'Of course!' said the pixies, at once. 'Where would you like them?'

'On our hindlegs, I think,' said the bee. 'It would be eazzzy to put the pollen there!'

So Snippit and Trim set to work and made clever little pockets for each of the bees, and put them neatly on their hindlegs. The bees were delighted, and flew off at once to collect pollen.

The pixies' pockets were just right. The bees packed them full of pollen and then flew off to the hive. How all the other bees envied them when they saw their new and useful pockets. You can guess that one by one they flew off to Snippit and Trim and asked for pockets, too.

And now every bee has pockets on its hindlegs and packs the pollen neatly there. Don't you believe me? Well, see for yourself!

ISBN 0-86163-807-7

Text copyright Darrell Waters Limited
Illustrations copyright © 1996 Award Publications Limited

Enid Blyton's signature is a trademark of Darrell Waters Limited

The Enchanted Gloves first published in *Sunny Stories for Little Folk 1926–1936*
Pixie Pockets first published 1941 by Evans Bros in *Enid Blyton's Book of the Year*

This edition first published 1996 by Award Publications Limited,
27 Longford Street, London NW1 3DZ

Printed in Italy